# MOUSE'S Christmas Wish

MOUSE'S
CHRISTMAS
W    I    S    H
A  PICTURE  CORGI
BOOK 978 0 552 56324 6
First        published        in
Great  Britain  by  Picture  Corgi,
an      imprint      of      Random
House          Children's          Books
A    Random    House    Group    Company
This edition  published 2011
1   3   5   7   9   10   8   6   4   2
Text   copyright   ©   Judi   Abbot   &
Random  House  Children's  Books,  2011
Illustrations  copyright  ©  Judi    Abbot,  2011
The right of Judi Abbot to be identified as the author
and  illustrator  of  this  work  has  been  asserted  in
accordance  with  the  Copyright,  Designs  and  Patents  Act  1988.
All rights reserved. No part of this publication may be reproduced,
stored   in   a   retrieval   system,   or   transmitted   in   any   form
or      by      any      means,      electronic,
mechanical,      photocopying,      recording
or  otherwise,    without  the  prior  permission
of  the  publishers.      Picture  Corgi  Books  are
published    by    Random    House    Children's    Books,
61-63        Uxbridge        Road,        London        W5        5SA
w w w . k i d s a t r a n d o m h o u s e . c o . u k
w w w . r a n d o m h o u s e . c o . u k
Addresses    for    companies    within    The    Random    House    Group
Limited    can    be    found    at:    www.randomhouse.co.uk/offices.htm
THE      RANDOM      HOUSE      GROUP      Limited      Reg.      No.      954009
A   CIP   catalogue
record     for     this
book   is   available
from    the    British
Library. Printed and
bound    in    China.

# MOUSE'S Christmas Wish

## Judi Abbot

PICTURE CORGI

*to Nico and Veri,*
*with love and fun!*

It was very nearly Christmas and Rabbit
was sending invitations to all her friends.
'One each for Duck and Bear, Dog and Mole
and, of course, one for Mouse.'

The next morning, in a little house deep in the forest, an invitation arrived, and it said:

Dear Mouse,
Please come and spend Christmas with me. Come as soon as you can.
Love Rabbit.
x x x

'Hurray!' shouted Mouse. 'That's just how I wished I'd be spending Christmas. Now, I've got so much to do before I can set off on the journey to Rabbit's house.'

On the furthest edge of the lake, Bear had also received an invitation.
'Whoopee!' he yelled. 'I'm on my way!'
He hurriedly threw some things into a
bag and set off.

High up on the top of the big snowy hill,
another invitation had arrived.
'Ah-ha,' smiled Dog. 'Now I can
try out my new sledge.'

Over on the other side of the lake, Duck was
already very busy. 'I need to bake a cake,
a pudding, pies, tarts and sweets. . .
I can't wait to spend Christmas
at Rabbit's house!'

And down at the railway station, standing on the platform,
Mole was already waiting for his train.
'How nice,' he said. 'I shall enjoy spending
Christmas with my friends.'

Meanwhile, Mouse had started packing.
'I'll need clothes for cold weather and warm, and for rain and snow.
And I'll take towels and sheets, some blankets, pans and plates,
extra shoes, hats and scarves…'

POP!

But the suitcase popped open. It just wouldn't stay shut.
'Oh no,' squealed Mouse. 'How am I going to carry it all?'

Bear had set out across the lake.
He loved to skate and he was
very good at it.

'What a pleasant journey,' thought Mole
as he gazed out of the train window.

Meanwhile, as Mouse went to wash up the breakfast things, he tripped over his suitcase and went flying!

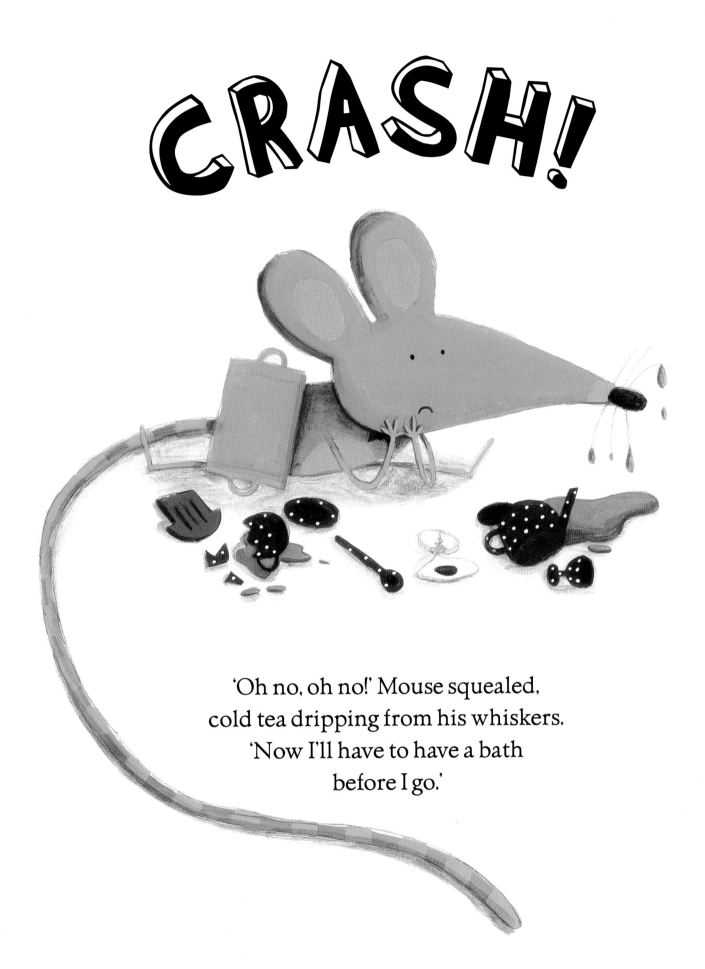

# CRASH!

'Oh no, oh no!' Mouse squealed,
cold tea dripping from his whiskers.
'Now I'll have to have a bath
before I go.'

Dog tore down
the big snowy hill
on his sledge,
ears flying.

'Wheeeee!'
he cried.

And at the bottom,
Duck was waiting.
'At last,' she thought.
'Here he is.
Hurry up, Dog!'

Meanwhile, Mouse had finally
finished packing when…

Drip

Drip

Drip

'The bath!' he yelled.
'I forgot about the bath!'
Poor Mouse, there was an awful
lot of mopping up to do.

Rabbit was busy too, getting everything ready.
'I hope they arrive soon, then we can decorate the tree and
hang up our stockings. What a wonderful Christmas this will be.'

Bear and Dog and Duck and Mole
were very nearly there. It wouldn't
be long before they all arrived,

all except...

Poor Mouse. He had finally set out, but it was snowing
so heavily he could hardly move, and it was starting
to get dark. He was beginning to feel scared.
'Oh, I wish I was already at Rabbit's house,' he squeaked.

Suddenly…

WHOMP!

a great pile of snow dropped off a branch.
'Help!' came the muffled cry.

By now all the others had arrived
at Rabbit's house.
'Ah, here you are!' she beamed.
'Now Christmas can really begin.'

Meanwhile, Mouse had dug
himself out of the snow. But it was dark
and he was cold and wet.

'It's impossible,' he sobbed. 'I just can't go on.
It's too far, it's too late. And all I wished for was
to spend Christmas with my friends.'
Slowly he trudged home, back
through the snow.

His friends were having a wonderful time.
They hung up the decorations, placed the
presents under the tree and put all
the tasty treats out on plates.

'But where is Mouse?' asked Rabbit.
'Wherever can he have got to?'

Mouse had gone to bed.

'My Christmas wish will
never come true now.'
His tears fell as he pulled the
covers over his head.

Just then there was a ring at the door.

'Oh dear, oh dear, who
can that be?' Mouse sniffed.
'It's too late for the postman
and it's not early enough
for the milkman.'

'SURPRISE!' everyone yelled.
'Come on, Mouse, you're late. We've come
to take you to Rabbit's house for Christmas.'

And they walked
to the end of
the lane,

past the old
fir tree,

round the
corner,

and there was
Rabbit's house.

'Whatever took you so long?' asked Mole.
'You practically live on Rabbit's doorstep!'

'Now we can really start enjoying Christmas,' said Rabbit. And everyone agreed. They sang songs, played games, ate treats and told stories.

'Ahem,' said Mouse. 'My dear friends, I thought my Christmas wish would never come true. Thank you for making this the best Christmas ever.'

Later that night, Mouse was
woken by a magical sound.
Shooting across the sky was
the one final visitor everyone
wishes to see at Christmas.

Happy Christmas, Mouse!